Table of Contents

Translator's Preface i
Dramatis Personae 1
Act I 2
   I. i 2
Act II 7
   II. i 7
   II. ii 9
Act III 18
   III. i 18
   III. ii 19
   III. iii 24
Act IV 28
   IV. i 28
   IV. ii 30
   IV. iii 38
Act V 42
   V. i 42
   V. ii 43
   V. iii 45

Translator's Preface

Seneca's *Thyestes* is a majestic yet challenging tragedy. The foremost difficulty in translating and even in simply reading his play for the first time is orienting oneself and grasping the mythological context of the play. His dark and moody depiction of the horrors of House Atreides advances along at quick clip from the inciting scenes of the underworld to a Mycenae torn by civil war and longing for peace to its dire conclusion in the grim banquet hall of the palace. The Atreides' calamitous descent into murder and mayhem accelerates from the opening scenes till the collision at the very end of the play, and Seneca achieves this frantic acceleration by omitting nearly all background information about the Atreides' legacy. The play opens in the bowels of the underworld with Tantalus long after he has murdered his son Pelops and fed him to the gods, and it offers no explicit description or biography of the nefarious grandfather or his brood. Instead Seneca makes only passing references to the already committed black deeds of Tantalus, his son Pelops, and his grandchildren Atreus and Thyestes so that the play focuses solely upon the family's final descent into ruin and so that the family plunges into the abyss rather than lurches.

Before the play opens, Tantalus has already slain his son Pelops, prepared his child as a culinary dish and served him to the Olympian gods, who were his intimate friends, in an effort to spite them. In response the gods sentenced Tantalus to the underworld where, in the opening scene of the play, we find him being tortured by perpetual thirst and food. Placed in a pool of water with the branches of a fruit tree, heavy with fruit, hanging above his head, Tantalus was able to reach neither the food nor the water which lay so close at hand.

    The gods, however, did not simply punish Tantalus, but they also saved Tantalus by reconstituting his body. When he reached manhood, Pelops became king of Pisa once he defeated the king Oenomaus in a murderous chariot race and won the hand of Oenomaus's daughter. Pelops was able to defeat Oenomaus because he conspired with Oenomaus's chariot driver Myrtilus; however, after he had become king, Pelops murdered Myrtilus by pushing him off a cliff into the sea. As he plummeted into the waters, Myrtilus invoked a curse upon Pelops and his family, and it is this curse which we see coming to fruition in *Thyestes*.

    Pelops and his wife Hippodamia had several children, but the most notable ones were Atreus and Thyestes whom the play centers around. In their youth Atreus and Thyestes conspired to murder their half-sibling Chrysippus so that he would not inherit the throne from Pelops, and they were exiled by their father in turn to Mycenae where they ascended to the throne together once the king of Mycenae died. While they ruled together, however, Thyestes seduced Atreus's wife and with her aid tricked his brother out of the throne. Thyestes's reign did not last long because, with the aid of the gods, Atreus was able to reclaim the throne and send Thyestes into exile. Seneca's play picks up at this point in the tragic history of the family, and so it is necessary for the reader to know all of this in order to fully understand the play.

I have used the Perseus edition of the Latin text. In my translation of *Thyestes*, I have omitted explanatory footnotes or endnotes so that the reader is not distracted from the play itself, and I have attempted to relay the play by using elevated yet not antiquated words and phrases so that the gravity of Seneca's Latin is reflected. Where I was able to retain his syntax without creating unrecognizable sentences, I did, and so my reader will find a multitude of passive voice constructions and dense sentences filled with dependent clauses and participial phrases. I have retained these for two reasons: first I would like the reader to hear as much of Seneca's voice as a translation can offer, and second I believe that his syntax and structure was intentionally chosen with poetic and philosophic ends in mind.

I would like to thank Melissa Parlin for first introducing me to Seneca's plays. While I knew Seneca the philosopher, I did not know Seneca the playwright before I assisted with one of her classes. She taught the

Medea so well that I promptly brought a two volume edition of his plays and devoured them. A few years later I took up the task of translating *Thyestes*, and the final product stands before my reader. I would also like to thank my loving wife for her support throughout my work.

Dramatis Personae

The Ghost of Tantalus, *grandfather of Atreus and Thyestes who is doomed to Tartarus for his sins*

A Fury, *a mythological being who punishes the wicked*

Chorus, *a group of Mycenaean citizens*

Atreus, *king of Mycenae and brother of Thyestes*

Attendant of Atreus

Thyestes, *brother of Atreus*

Three sons of Thyestes, *Tantalus, Plisthenes and Tacitus of whom only Tantalus speaks*

A Messenger

Act I

I. i

The shade of Tantalus and a Fury enter in Hades.

The Ghost of Tantalus: Who drags the man begging for fleeing food in his greedy maw from his unfortunate seat of hell? Which of the gods wickedly shows hated homes to Tantalus again? Has anything worse been found than being parched with thirst in the waves and being open-mouthed with famine always? Surely Sisyphus's stone, about to be carried with my slick shoulders, or the wheel separating limbs with its swift running, or the punishment of Tityus, who lying in a deserted cave feeds the black birds his entrails which have been poured forth and which at night are repaired and who afterward lies down as plump fodder for the monster on the fresh day? Will I be led to this evil? O whatever it be, hard master of the damned, you appoint new punishments for each one which has been executed; if anything is able to be added to those punishments, which the guard of this dire prison shudders at, which gloomy Acheron is terrified at, the fear of which I also tremble at, search for it. Now the crowd of shades assumes a form from my race who surpasses his family and makes me seem innocent and who dares that which ought not to be dared. Whatever impious region of this place is free from my descendants, I will fill; while the House of Pelops stands, Minos will never be idle.

Fury: Go on, detestable shade, and drive your impious family to the Furies. Let it compete in every wicked deed, and let the sword be drawn in alternating turns, and let there be neither a limit of anger nor shame; let blind madness urge their minds; let the madness of the parents endure, and let their boundless sin go to the grandchildren; and let not this ancient crime be idle for anyone to hate it: let a new crime always arise, and let not one sin arise in another while it is being punished. Let kingdoms depart from the proud brothers, and let them recall the exiles: between the uncertain kings let the uncertain fortune of the violent house fall; from power let there be misery, from misery let there be power, and let chance with her unremitting wave carry the kingdom. On account of these sins, they will be driven out; let them return to their sins when the gods return their country to them, and let them be hated by all men more than they hate themselves; let there be nothing which rage thinks is forbidden: let brother be frightened of brother, and let he, who has been born, fear his father; let the children die evilly, but let them be conceived in greater evil; let the hostile wife threaten her husband; let wars pass the sea; let all of the blood, which will be poured out, irrigate the lands; let conquering desire triumph over the great leaders of the nations. Let dishonor be very trivial in the impious home; may both the divine law and trust and the right of a brother pass away. May heaven not be free from your evil deeds—why do the stars glitter in heaven; why do the flames preserve the glory owed to the world? Let the night become different; let day perish from heaven. Confound the household gods; summon hatred, murder and corpses, and fill up the house with Tantalus. Let the heights be decorated, and let the happy doors turn green with laurel; let a worthy fire begin to shine with your arrival; let the evil deeds of the Thracians become greater in number. Why is the uncle's hand idle? Has Thyestes yet wept for his children? When will he destroy them? Let the copper pots foam with [Canibal] the applied fires; let their limbs, once they have been plucked off, go in by parts; let their blood pollute the hearths of the fatherland; let the dinner courses be drawn up—you will come as a table companion to some evil deed not new to you. We gave you a free day, and we loosed your hunger at these tables of yours; finish your fasting; let the gore, which has been mixed into the wine be drank by you as you watch; come to the feasts which you would flee—stop; where do you rush headlong to?

The Ghost of Tantalus: To the pools and the rivers and the retreating waters and the retreat of the abundant tree from my lips themselves. Allow me to return to the black den of my prison; if I do not seem miserable enough, let me be permitted to change shores: let me be abandoned in your riverbed, Phlethegon, surrounded by your burning seas. What punishments, which have been given by the law of the Fates, you are ordered to suffer, whoever lies beneath a tomb, which has been swallowed up, terrified and fearful of the collapse of the mountain, which will come, whoever dreads the savage jaws of ravenous lions and the dire columns of the Furies, whoever, half-burnt, drives away their firebrands, which have been thrown, hear the voice of hastening Tantalus: believe me, an expert; love your punishments. When will I be allowed to flee the gods on high?

[margin: Punishment is their fate]

Fury: First disturb your household, and bring battles and the evil love of the sword to the kings; upset the wild heart with a raging commotion.

[margin: wants their minds mad with violence]

The Ghost of Tantalus: It is fitting that I suffer a punishment, not that I am a punishment. Am I sent as a dire vapor to sprinkle a grave sickness on my people? Will I a grandfather lead my grandchildren into horrible sin? Great father of the gods and us, however much it shames you, although my talkative

[margin: on his family]

[margin: believes not right to inflict punishment]

won't do it - won't be silent even if he gets punished

tongue suffers a grievous fixed punishment, I will
not be silent in this matter: I warn you: neither
violate your sacred hands with gore, nor sprinkle
your altars with avenging evil. I will stand and hinder
this evil deed. Why do you terrify my face with your
whip, and why do you brandish twisted snakes? Why
do you rouse an imposed hunger in my inmost parts?
My heart, burnt with thirst, blazes, and the flame
darts in my in burnt innards. I follow you.

telling his family to not commit evil

trying to prevent madness and wickedness

being tortured? giving in?

Fury: Divide this madness into your whole house.
Thus, thus let them suffer, and let them, enraged,
each in turn thirst for blood. The house knows your
comings, and it shudders in every part at your evil
touch. The deed is more than enough. Go to your
infernal caves and familiar river; now the mournful
land reluctantly bears your step; do you discern that
water, since it has been driven inward, forsakes the
springs so that the banks are empty and the fiery
winds bring thin clouds? Every tree grows pale, and
the naked branch thirsts while its fruit is fleeing. The
Isthmus roars with nearby waves, dividing the nearby
channels with slender lands, but it hears the remote
sound from afar. Now the Lerna has withdrawn
backwards, and the Phoronides has returned to its
fissures, and the sacred Alpheos does not send forth
its waters, and the ridges of Cithaeron stand while no
white snow has been deposited on that region, and

make them craving each other blood

ghost of T has evil touch

the nobles of Argos fear the ancient drought? Behold the sun, a titan, himself considers whether he will order the day, which is about to perish, to follow, or whether he will compel it to go with his reins.

Act II

II. i

In Argos a chorus of Mycenaean citizens enters.

Chorus: If anyone loves the Pisaean homes of the Isthmus, famed in Achaia for their chariots, if anyone loves the kingdom of Corinth and its twin gates and the separating sea, if any summer loosens the famous snows, which Sarmatian Boreas winds made with a cold season on all the peaks with Etesian winds of Taygetus which the clear Alpheos touches with its frozen river, let Argos, known for the Olympic stadium, encounter a peaceful divine will from the gods, and let it ward off another evil lest conspiracies return, the more evil grandson succeed his grandfather, and a greater guilt please the descendants. At last let Tantalus's impious and weary progeny, who has been cast out, depart from his wild attempts. His sin is enough; common right or wrong has not prevailed; Myrtilus, the deceiver of his lord, after he himself had been betrayed, died, and he, having been cast down by the faith by which he had become respected, rendered the sea with a changed name: no tale is more known to Ionian sailors. Tantalus, a little child, taken out by your impious sword, while he ran toward the kisses of his father, fell as an untimely sacrifice at the altars, and he was divided at the tables by your right hand so that you might provide for your guests the gods. Eternal hunger took vengeance on these foods; a more fitting punishment could not be decided for these savage foods. The tired Tantalus stands with an empty gullet; plentiful booty, fleeing faster than Phineas's birds, hang over his noxious head; a tree broods here and there with swollen boughs, and the tree, bent with fruit and trembling, frolics with his wide open jaws. However, hungry and intolerant of delay, he, because he has been deceived so many times, neglects to touch these things, and he strains his eyes, and he squeezes his mouth, and he impedes his hunger with his closed teeth, but then the whole grove drops all its riches , and the sweet ripe fruits leap down from above from the languid leaves, and they inflame his hunger, which commands his ineffective hands to move—when he brought forth his hands and was pleased to be deceived, the whole harvest is snatched into a high place, and then a thirst not lighter than the hunger approaches; when his blood has warmed and kindled with these fiery brands, he stands miserable seeking the hostile waves with his mouth, from which the fleeing waters withdraw, disappointing with its sterile waters, and it departs as he attempts to follow; this man drinks deeply the dust from the rapid whirlpool.

II. ii

Atreus and an attendant enter in the royal palace

Atreus: Lazy, inactive, powerless and that which I deem to be the most disgraceful for a king, unavenged, Atreus, after so much wickedness, after the schemes of your brother and after every one of heaven's laws has been destroyed, do you angry Atreus spend your time in vain complaints? The whole world ought to be roaring against your arms, and it was fitting that your ships sail to both sides of the twin seas; already you ought to have lit fields and cities with flames and to have flashed a drawn sword everywhere; the whole land of Argos sings beneath our cavalry; let neither forests hide our enemy nor fortresses constructed on the lofty heights of mountains; let the entire populace, after they have departed Mycenae, sing for war; let whoever hides his hated head fall in a calamitous slaughter; let this the strong house itself of famed Pelops be ruined, or let it fall on me provided that it falls on my brother. Come my soul, do that which none of my posterity will approve but which none will be silent about; some savage bloodthirsty evil deed must be dared—

[margin note: & his crime will be avenged by a worse crime]

such that my brother would prefer that it was his—unless you have excelled them, you have not avenged evils; what even is able to be so savage that it overcomes him? Surely he does not lie down humbled? Surely he does not suffer rule in these favorable things, rest in these tired things. I understand the unteachable nature of that man; he cannot be persuaded—he can be broken. So then before he forms himself or prepares his forces, let him be attacked wantonly lest he attack me while I am resting. Either he will destroy, or he will be destroyed: in between us an evil deed has been placed for one of us to claim.

[margin note: before he recovers, attack him]

Attendant: Does not an unfavorable reputation with the people terrify you?

Atreus: This is the greatest good of a kingdom: that the people are so coerced that as they suffer the deeds of their lord they praise those same acts.

Attendant: Fear compels some to praise, and it renders the same ones hostile, but he, who seeks the glory of true favor, will wish to be praised in the mind more than by voice.

Atreus: True praise often reaches even the humble man, but false praise does not reach anyone except the powerful. Let the powerful will that which others do not.

Attendant: Let a king desire honest things: no one will not wish for the same.

Atreus: Wherever only honesty is permitted to the ruler, there he is master only by a prayer.

Attendant: Where there is no shame and there is no administration of justice, no sanctity, no piety, and no trust, royal power is unstable.

Atreus: Sanctity, piety and trust are private goods; let kings go where they please. [*are for subjects / Kings can act as they want / do whatever*]

Attendant: Consider it evil to harm even an evil brother. [*Surely its wrong to harm a bad man?*]

[*whatever is wrong is right*]

Atreus: Whatever is evil in regard to a brother is good in regard to that man. For what has he left untouched by crime, or where has he refrained from evil? He took away my wife with adultery and my kingdom with a trick; he gained the ancient symbol of rule with deceit; he threw my home into confusion by fraud; there is in the lofty stables of Tantalus's noble flock, a secret ram, the leader of that opulent flock; the hair of this beast hangs down flowing with gold over its entire body; from his back the new kings of Tantalus's house have their gilded scepters: the owner of this thing rules; the fortune of so great a house follows this man; the sacred ram grazes in a secluded part in guarded meadows which stone

[*riddled with revenge*]

encloses, defending the pasture with the fateful rocky wall. Once he had dared this monstrous crime, he, that faithless one, departed with the consort of my bedchamber who had been caught up in his crime. The whole evil of our mutual ruin flowed from this: I, a frightened exile, wandered through my kingdom; no part of my family is safe and free from these treacheries; my wife had been corrupted; trust in my authority was shaken; my house is ill; my blood is doubtful—nothing is certain except that my brother is my enemy; what are you shocked? At last begin and take up these spirits: Tantalus and Pelops—look to them; my hands are demanded for these works of theirs. Declare the profane thing: by what path I will destroy that head.

Attendant: Once he has been destroyed by the sword, let him spew forth his hostile soul.

Atreus: You speak about the conclusion of the punishment; I wish for a punishment. Let a mild tyrant kill; let death be begged for in my kingdom.

Attendant: Does no pity move you?

Atreus: Withdraw, pity, but only if you ever were in my house; let the horrible cohort of the Furies, let the warring Furies and let Megara, shaking her twin brands, come; my heart does not burn with a great

12

[margin note: wants to know what Atreus is planning]

enough madness; it delights to be filled with a greater monstrosity.

Attendant: What new thing do you in your madness craft?

Atreus: Nothing, which the rule of accustomed indignation comprehends; I will forsake no crime, and none is satisfactory. *— now is bad enough*

Attendant: The sword?

Atreus: It is not enough

Attendant: What of fire?

Atreus: It is still not enough.

Attendant: Then what weapon will your great anguish use?

Atreus: Thyestes himself.

Attendant: This evil is greater than your rage.

Atreus: I admit it. An astonished confusion shakes and stirs deep within my feelings; I am carried away, and I do not know where, but I am being carried away. No, rather the ground bellows from its foundation, and the clear day thunders, and the house cracks as if the entire roof had been broken, and the upset Lares turn away their faces; let this thing be done; let an evil deed, which the gods will fear, be done.

Attendant: What are you at last planning to do?

Atreus: I do not know what thing, greater and more expansive than custom, beyond the limits of human mores, swells up in my mind and is near my slow hands—I do not know what it may be, but it will be something powerful. May it be so. Soul, seize this thing. It is a crime worthy of Thyestes and worthy of Atreus: each may do this; the Thracian house has seen tables of abominable things—I confess; the crime is inhuman, but it has been done; let pain find anything greater than this; Daulian parent and daughter, inspire my mind; our motive is similar; attend and urge my hand; let the lustful father, as he is rejoicing, mangle his sons and eat their limbs. It is well it is more than enough. This way of punishment is pleasing; where in the world is he? Why does Atreus live for so long innocent? The whole image of slaughter now wanders before my eyes; lost children thrust into the mouth of their father—soul, what do you fear in return, and do you sink before the deed? Come, it must be risked: he himself will do that which is the special sin in that crime.

Attendant: But with what tricks will he be captured and induced to put his foot into our snares? He believes that we are all enemies.

Atreus: He cannot be captured unless he wishes to capture. Now he hopes for my kingdom: in this hope he will resist Jove although he threatens with his bolt; in this hope he will overcome the threat of a swollen stream and the dangerous sea of Libyan sand; in this hope he will see what he deems to be the greatest evil, his brother.

Attendant: Who give him the confidence of peace? Whom will he believe about such a thing?

Atreus: Shameless hope is gullible. Moreover, to my children I will give the commission which they will bring to their uncle: that the exile, roving from his remaining lodgings, exchange miseries for a kingdom and rule Argos from his office of lord; if he spurns my requests too much, they will move his wild children who are tired from grave evils and are ready to be captured by a request: here the ancient love of our kingdom and in that place their sad poverty and hard suffering will subjugate the man no matter how hard he is from so many evils.

Attendant: Time has already made his afflictions light.

Atreus: You are wrong; his sense of the wrongs grows each day. To bear woes is light; to endure them till the end is onerous.

Attendant: Choose other ministers of your sad plan.

Atreus: Young men hear rather evil lessons easily.

Attendant: They will do to their father whatever you teach them to do to their uncle: the evil deeds often return to their teacher.

Atreus: Although no one teaches them the ways of fraud and evil, the kingdom will teach them; do you fear that they will become evil? They were born. That which you call savage and cruel and which you believe to be done too harshly and impiously is perhaps even done there by him.

Attendant: Will the children know that this fraud is being prepared?

Atreus: There is no silent loyalty in such undeveloped years; perhaps they will uncover my plans; to be silent is learned through the many evils of life.

Attendant: Do you even deceive the very ones whom you intend to use to deceive another?

Atreus: In this way they will be removed from the crime and the guilt: for why is it necessary to plant my children into evil? Let my hatred display itself through itself. –You do poorly; you ebb, my soul: if you spare your children, you will spare those children; let Agamemnon become a minister of my plan, and let Menelaus, knowing, aid his father; let the uncertainty of their birth be answered with this evil deed: if they reject war and do not wish to carry on my hatred, if they call him uncle, he is their father. Let it pass.—Nervous expressions are accustomed to reveal many things, but great plans also reveal the unwilling: let them not know of how great a matter they ministers; you will conceal my plans.

Attendant: I should not need to be warned: that confidence of yours and my fear but even more my loyalty will shut them up in my heart.

Act III

III. i

Enter the Chorus

Chorus: At last our noble kingdom, the race of ancient Inachus has settled the threats of the brothers. What madness stirs you all to spill each other's blood in turn and to seize the scepter with a crime? You all, who are greedy for the heights, do not know where royal power lies. Resources do not make a king; nor do clothes of Tyrian color, nor the mark of a royal brow, nor vessels shining with gold: a king is he who has laid down the fears and dreadful evils of his heart; whom impotent ambition does not move and whom the steadfast favor of the dangerous commons never moves; nor whatever golden things the West digs up or the Tagus turns up with its golden wave in its famous channel; nor whatever the seething threshing floor treads out in the Libyan harvests; whom the falling path of the slanting lightning will not shake; nor Eurus seizing the sea nor the raging swollenness of the windy Adriatic with its savage straits whom neither the soldiers lance nor drawn steel has subdued; who, because he has been placed in a secure place, sees everything below himself and meets his fate cheerfully and does not protest against death. Although kings who control the scattered Dahae, who far and wide hold the shoals of the Red

Sea and the blood sea with its many gems or who open the ridges of Caspia to the Sarmatians, come together, although a king, who dares to despoil the noble Seres wherever they lie, compete, a good mind will rule the kingdom. That king has no need for horses or arms or the weak arrows which Parthia hurls from afar while they pretend to flee; he has no need for machines which have been drawn up to scatter cities, whirling stones from afar. A king is he, who fears nothing; a king is he who will desire nothing; whoever this is gives the kingdom to himself. Let whoever will wish it stand powerful on the slippery height of royal power: may sweet repose satisfy me; since I have been placed in an obscure station, may I be satisfied by sweet repose; may my lifetime, known by none of my fellow citizens, flow in silence. Thus, when my days go over with no uproar, I will die an old plebeian. Death lies heavy on the one who dies, known too much by all but unknown to himself.

Chorus exits

III. ii

Thyestes, Tantalus, Plisthenes, and Tacitus, his three sons, enter the countryside of Argos.

Thyestes: I see the welcomed homes of my fatherland, the riches of the Argives, the land of my birth, which is the greatest good for miserable exiles, the paternal gods (if there are still gods), the sacred towers of the Cyclopes, glories greater than human labor, and the racetrack, celebrated by the young men and on which I as a noble have carried the palm in my father's chariot not merely one time. Argos will meet me; its numerous people will meet me, but of course Atreus will also come. Rather return to wooded exile and the dense woodlands and to a life mixed up with and similar to the beasts. This famous splendor of the throne is not such that it should carry off my eyes with its false glory: when you look at a gift, gaze even upon its giver. Only among those things, which everyone considers difficult, have I been happy and strong; on the contrary now I am thrown back into fears; my soul hesitates, and it desires to draw its body backwards; I make an unwilling step.

Tantalus: What can this mean? My father advances with a slow gait as if he is stunned, and he turns his face and holds an uncertain direction.

Thyestes: Why, my soul, do you hesitate, or why do you consider for so long an easy plan? Do you fear very uncertain things, your brother and the kingdom; do you fear evils which have already been tamed and overcome; do you flee from toils which have been well settled? It helps to be poor already; turn back your feet while you are allowed, and rescue yourself.

Tantalus: What cause compels you, father, to retrace your step from the country which you have seen? Why do you withdraw your bosom from such goods? Your brother relents from his anger, which has been cast away, and he returns your part of the kingdom. He composes the frame of the mangled house, and he has restored you to yourself.

Thyestes: You weigh a cause of fear which I myself do not know. I see nothing which should be feared, yet I fear nonetheless. To go pleases me, but I totter on uncertain knees. In the same way as the sea subduing a ship which hastens with oarsmen and sail, forces back the sail and oarsmen, I, abducted, am brought to some place other than where I am struggling to go.

Tantalus: Subdue whatever hinders you and impedes your courage, and consider your return and whatever gifts await you. Father, you can rule.

Thyestes: Because I am able to die.

Tantalus: The highest power is—

Thyestes: Nothing if you desire nothing.

Tantalus: You will bequeath it to your sons.

Thyestes: A throne does not hold two.

Tantalus: Does he, who is able to be happy, prefer to be miserable?

Thyestes: Believe me; distinguished things please with false names; hard things are feared in vain. While I stood exalted, I never ceased to be frightened and to fear the very sword at my side. O how good it is to oppose no one, to grasp safe meals while I recline on the ground! Evils do not enter into huts, and safe food is held on a narrow table; poison is drunk in gold—I, who am experienced, speak: it is alright to prefer bad fortune to good. The lowly citizen does not shake at my secure and lofty house on a high mountain; splendid ivory does not shine from my lofty roof, and a watchman does not defend my sleep. We do not fish from fleets, and we do not drive the sea backwards with a constructed dam. We do not feed a greedy belly with the tribute of the nations; let no field beyond the Getans and the Parthians be reaped for me; we are not honored with frankincense, nor are my altars adorned after Jove has been excluded. No forest has been planted on my heights, and many baths, which have been heated by hand, do not produce steam for me. Day is not given to sleep, and restless night is not yoked to Bacchus:

but we are not afraid. Our home is safe without a weapon, and great rest is available in small things. To be able to endure without a kingdom is an immense kingdom.

Tantalus: If god gives an empire, it must not be refused, and it must not be sought. Your brother asks that you rule.

Thyestes: He asks? He must be feared. Some deceit wanders here.

Tantalus: Loyalty is accustomed to return to where it has been driven from, and just affections repair those powers which have been lost.

Thyestes: My brother loves Thyestes? First the North Sea will flood the heavens and the grasping wave of the Sicilian tide will stand still, and then ripe grain will rise from the Ionian Sea. Black night will give light to the lands; first waters will be joined with flames; life will be joined with death, and wind will join faith and treaty with the sea.

Tantalus: But what crime do you fear?

Thyestes: All of them: what limit will I set for my dread? He is capable of as much as he hates.

Tantalus: What is he capable of against you?

Thyestes: Now I fear nothing for myself: you all make Atreus frightening to me.

Tantalus: Now that you have been made safe, are you afraid of being cheated?

[margin note: worried Atreus will hurt his children]

Thyestes: In the midst of evils, it is too late to be cautious: it is past. But I, your father, swear this one thing: I follow you all, I do not lead you.

Tantalus: God will provide for those things which you have considered; do not proceed with uncertain steps.

Thyestes and his sons exit.

III. iii

Atreus, Thyestes, Tantalus, Plisthenes, and Tacitus enter.

Atreus *(aside):* The enclosed wild beast is held by the set traps: I see both the man himself and at the same time the innate quality of his hated stock joined to their parent; my hatreds now dwell in a safe place. At last Thyestes has come into my hands, and even every part of him has come. I scarcely temper my soul; resentment barely holds the reins. It is just as when the keen scented hunting dog, tracking beasts and held by a long leash, searches the paths with its lowered mouth; while far off it perceives the swine

[margin note: can barely control his anger]

with its easy odor, it obeys and roams the place with its silent mouth; when the prey is closer, the hound fights with its whole head and calls with a whine to its master standing behind it, and it snatches itself away from the man restraining it. While anger hope for blood, it forgets to be hidden, but let it be hidden. Look how his heavy hair covers up his gloomy expressions with its filth; how his filthy beard lies. Let trust prevail— *(to Thyestes)* it is delightful to see my brother; return your longed for embraces to me. Whatever belonged to anger, let it pass; let family and duty be cherished from this day forward; let damned hatreds depart from our souls.

Thyestes: I might explain away everything if you were not such a man. But I confess, Atreus, I confess; I admit everything which you believe. Today's goodness has made my cause very evil. Whatever seems harmful to so good a brother is utterly criminal. Tears must be spent: you first will see me as a suppliant; these uncompromised hands will plead to you at your feet; let all your anger be laid aside, and let the infection, once it has been cleaned from your soul, disappear. Receive these innocents as pledges of my faith, brother.

Atreus: Take your hands from my knees, and seek my embrace instead. You all also, so young and the refuge of the aged, hang from my neck. Take off your filthy garment, and spare my eyes, and once you have been richly adorned, claim my companions, and happily take part of your brother's empire. This greater glory is mine: to return paternal glory to my unharmed brother; to have a kingdom is an accident, to give one is excellence.

Thyestes: May the gods weigh out an equal reward to you for such service, brother. You all occupy a famous palace; our squalor rejects it, and my unlucky hand flees from the scepter. Let me be permitted to hide in the commons.

Atreus: The throne admits two.

Thyestes: Whatever is yours, brother, I believe is mine.

Atreus: Who refuses the gifts of flowing fortune?

Thyestes: Whoever has experienced how easily they flow.

Atreus: Do you forbid your brother to obtain immense glory?

Thyestes: Your glory has already been completed; mine remains: to reject the throne is sure counsel for me.

Atreus: I will leave mine behind unless you accept your share.

Thyestes: I accept: I will endure the title of an imposed kingdom, but the laws and arms with me will serve you.

Atreus: Bear the imposed chains on your soon to be venerated head. I will give the appointed sacrifices.

All exit.

Act IV

IV. i

Chorus: Does anyone believe this? Ferocious Atreus, that wild beast not powerful of mind, hesitates because he has been stunned by the appearance of his brother. No force is greater than true piety: hostile quarrels endure for strangers; those, whom true love has held, it will hold. Anger, which has been stirred up by great causes, destroys friendships and shouts for war. Troops with horses are heard; the stirred up sword, which raging Mars, desiring fresh blood, moves in a metrical beat, flashes here and there. Piety will overwhelm the sword with joined hands and will lead scoffers to peace. What god made such calm out of the uproar? The drums of civil war rang out just now through Mycenae: pale mothers held their sons; wives feared for their armed husbands when the unwilling sword, dirty with the ruin of restful peace. That one strove to rebuild falling walls, this one to strengthen towers weakened with neglect, another to restrain gates with iron bars. And the panicked watch of uneasy night broods on the parapets: the fear itself of war is worse than war. Now the threats of savage iron have fallen; now the heavy murmur of trumpets is silent; now the shriek of the resounding war horn is silent; high peace has been retrieved for the happy city. Thus

when the waves swelled from the deep, while the
Corus strikes the Bruttian Sea, Scylla resounds from
the beaten caverns, and sailors dread the sea in port
because rapacious Charybdis vomits out draughts,
and the Cyclops, while he resided on the cliff of
Aetna, feared his father: that the fire in the eternal
forges would be profaned by the spilled over waves,
and while Ithaca is trembling the poor man Laertes
thinks that his kingdom is able to be submerged. If
their strength has failed the winds, the sea reclines
more tranquil than a lagoon; the deeps, which a ship
feared to split, spectacular and spread out revealed
itself to playing skiffs with spread sail from here and
there, and it is idle to count up the immersed fish
here where troubled women just now feared the sea
beneath a huge gale. No fate is long; grief and
pleasure befall one in turn: pleasure is more brief. A
fickle hour swaps the lowest things for the highest:
that one, who bestows the diadem on the forehead,
before whom people leaned upon a knee, at whose
nod the Mede, the Indian of the nearer sun and the
Dahae, who threaten the Parthians with cavalry, lay
down their arm, anxiously holds the scepter. He
foresees and fears the changing fortunes, which
move all things, of affairs and uncertain time. You
all, to whom the ruler of sea and land gave the great
right of death and life, put off your expressions
puffed up with pride. Whatever your lesser fears

from you, your greater threatens to you; every throne is beneath a greater throne. The one, whom the coming day saw proud, the retreating day saw lying in ruin. Let no one trust too much to good fortune. Let no one despair of better things for the weary: Clotho mixes these things for those and forbids that Fortune stand still; every fate rotates; no one has so many blessings that he is able to promise himself tomorrow: the god spins our affairs, which have been set in motion, in a swift spiral.

IV. ii

(A messenger enters)

Messenger: Which whirlwind will bear me headlong through the clouds and wrap me in a dark cloud so that such an evil is snatched away from my eyes. The House of Pelops and even of Tantalus ought to be ashamed.

[margin note: ashamed of what Atreus has planned]

Chorus: What news do you bring?

Messenger: Which region do you refer to? Argos? Sparta which obtained loyal twins by lot? Corinth pressing the straits of the twin seas? Or the Hister presenting flight to the Alani? Or the Hyrcan land beneath the eternal snow, or that of the Scythians who wander everywhere? What place is witness to the monstrous evil here?

Chorus: Declare and unfold this evil whatever it is.

Messenger: If my soul should stand still, if my body, rigid with dread, should relax its members, I will. The image of the wild deed is stuck in my sight; bear me far away from that place, wild winds; bear me to that place where the day, carried off from here, is borne.

[margin note: Shaking with how horrific it is]

Chorus: You hold minds too gravely uncertain. Reveal that which you shudder at and its author: I do ask who it is, but which. Speak more quickly.

Messenger: In the highest citadel of Pelops, part of the home, whose outermost side is equal to a mountain and presses upon the city, is turned toward the southern winds; and it has a people stiff-necked towards their kings beneath its rule; here a huge and capacious room, whose noble columns with various spots bear beams gilded with gold, shines forth to the mob; after those things, known publically, which the people love, the wealthy home scatters into many areas; a secret area lies in the inmost secret place: in a low valley an ancient wood, confining the sanctuary of the household gods, lies, in which no tree is accustomed to offer happy boughs or to be cultivated by iron but the yew and the cypress and the forest with its black hidden ilex, above which an oak looks down from on high and excels the grove.

Here the Tantalid kings were accustomed to take the auspices; here they were accustomed with the offerings to search for power in slipping affairs and doubts; the chained offerings dwell here the vocal trumpets, the Myrtoan spoils of the conquered sea, and the wheels with their false axles hang there, and every crime of their family; in this place Pelops Phrygian turban, the spoils of his enemy and the embroidered mantle from his barbaric triumph are found.

A sad font stands beneath the gloom, and it slowly joins a black pool; such a stream is of the awful disfigured Styx which accomplishes pledges in heaven. In this place in the blind night there is a rumor that the gods of death groan; the grove resounds with clattered chains and the gods of the underworld howl. Whatever is dreadful to hear is seen in that place. An aged crowd, of those who have been expelled from their ancient tombs, wanders about, and monsters greater than those which are known spring forth in that place: in fact the sylvan roofs are accustomed to flash flames and the lofty trunks glow without fire. Often the grove bellows triple barking; often the home is astonished with great likenesses, and day does not settle the fear; night is special for the grove, and the superstition of the underworld rules in the light; in this place certain responses are given to the petitioners when the fates are loosened with a mighty sound in the innermost shrine, and the cave bellows while the god is loosening its voice. Where afterwards Atreus, raving and carrying the children of his brother, entered; the altars are adorned—who is able to describe this properly? He binds their noble hands behind the young men's backs, and he fastens their heads with a grim purple cord; the frankincense is not lacking nor the sacred liquid of Bacchus, nor the knife and the sacred meal touching the victim. Every order is served lest such an evil deed not be done rightly.

Chorus: Who applies his hand to the knife?

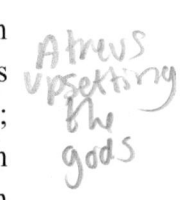

Messenger: He himself is the priest; he himself sings the fatal song in a calamitous prayer with his violent mouth; he himself stands at the altars; he himself caresses those ones devoted to death and takes up and draws near with the knife; he himself carefully attends: no part of the sacrifice goes to waste. The grove begins to tremble; the royal palace uncertain where it places its weight and with similar hesitations wavered with the whole ground shaken from below; a constellation ran dragging a black track out from the left side of the sky. The wine, once it has been poured out as a libation into the flames, flows as blood having been transformed from wine; twice and then a third time the royal crown falls from his head, and the ivory statues in the temple wept. The unnatural things moved everyone, but Atreus stood unmoved, and he frightens the gods wantonly warning him. And now, once the hindrance has been disregarded, he stands at the altars looking on grimly and obliquely. As the starving tigress in the Ganges forests vacillates between two young bulls, and desirous of the spoils from each yet uncertain where it will bring its jaws first (it turns its jaws on this one and turns them back on that one and keeps her uncertain hunger); thus awful Atreus watches their heads consecrated to his impious anger. He hesitates over which he will slaughter first for himself then which he will offer in the second sacrifice. And it does not concern him, but he hesitates, and he delights to order the wicked deed.

Chorus: But whom did he attack with his knife?

Messenger: The first spot, lest you think that his piety is lacking, is dedicated to his grandsire: Tantalus is his first sacrifice.

Chorus: With what courage, with what expression did he bear the murder?

Messenger: He stood free from self-concern, and he did not allow prayer vainly to be wasted; but the wild man buried his knife in that child's wound, and pressing deeply he joined his hand to the boy's neck.

[Margin notes: "gruesome imagery"; "how Atreus did it"; "Atreus like a lion"]

Once the blade had been withdrawn, the corpse stood, and after it had hesitated for a long time whether it would fall in this direction or that, it fell into its uncle. Then that wild man dragged Plisthenes to the altar, and he added him to his brother. He lopped off their pierced necks; once the neck had been hewn off, the trunk fell forward; the head rolled gasping a mournful sound with an unsure murmur.

Chorus: What then did he do, having finished the twin slaughter? Did he spare the boy, or did he heap evil deed upon evil deed?

Messenger: As a maned Armenian lion, triumphant in a wide slaughter, broods over the cattle (jaws dripping with gore and although his famine has been routed, he does not lay aside his violence: pressing the bulls here and there, he now lazily threatens the young bulls with lethargic jaws)—no differently Atreus raged, and his anger swelled until holding the blade wet with twin slaughter he, forgetting against whom he raged, with his dangerous hand drove it to the opposite side of his victim's body till the knife, taken in by the boy's chest, appeared out his back. That boy fell, and extinguishing the altar with the blood from both sides of the wound, he died.

Chorus: Oh cruel wicked deed!

Messenger: Have you ever been horrified? If the evil deed stood there, it would have been piety to that point.

Chorus: Does nature permit something beyond this: either greater or more terrible?

Messenger: Do you think this was the end of the evil deed? It was only a step.

Chorus: What was he capable of beyond this? Perhaps to be mangled, he threw the bodies to the wild animals, and he kept them from fire?

Messenger: If only he had kept it away! Let not the earth cover or fire scatter those things which have been performed. It is alright for the birds to feast upon them, and may he drag the sad substance to the wild beasts—that, which is accustomed to be a punishment, is a religious right compared to what he did. May the father see his unburied sons. O evil deed, unbelievable in any age and which posterity will deny! The entrails, taken from their living torsos, trembled, and their chests exhaled, and their frightened hearts leapt still; and he hauled out the scales and inspected the oracles, and he noted the still warm cavity of the entrails. After the victims satisfied him, he untroubled was idle till his brother's feast. At the right moment he divided the broken up bodies into parts; he lopped off the open arms up to the trunks, and he stern and thrifty stripped the hindrances of the muscles and removed the bones. He saved only the heads and hands which had been devoted to his pledge. These body parts were stuck on spits, and they were dropped into the slow ovens; the boiled water in those grumbling kettles tossed out the body parts. The fire leapt across those imposed foods, and once it had been returned twice and then thrice to the trembling hearth and been ordered to suffer delay there, it burned unwillingly. The food hissed on the spits, and I will not say easily whether the bodies or the flames groaned more. The fire died in pitch black smoke, and the smoke itself, a gloomy and heavy fog, did not rightly rise up, and it held itself at the ceiling. It invested the household gods themselves a deformed cloud.

O suffering Phoebus, although you fled backwards and buried the broken day in the afternoon, you fell too late. The father tore his children and chewed their sad bodies in his mouth; he sodden and heavy with wine slicked his hair with flowing oil; his closed throat often held the food. Thyestes, in an evil matter it is good for you that you are ignorant of your own evil deeds. But even this will pass: although the Titan himself, following the easy path, should turn his chariot, and heavy night, sent from the east at a strange time, should bury the foul deed with new shadows, it, however, must be seen. The whole evil affair will be uncovered.

Messenger exits.

IV. iii

Unnatural darkness falls upon the land.

Chorus: Where, father of the gods and the lands, whose whole splendor has fled at the rising of this dark night, where do you turn your course, and do you destroy day from the middle of Olympus? Why, Phoebus, do you snatch away your visage? Vesper, the messenger of the late hour, does not yet summons the nocturnal lights: the bend of the not yet western wheel orders that you release the veteran chariots; the third trumpet has not yet given the signal as the day inclines into light; the plowman with his not yet tired oxen is amazed at the time of unexpected dinner; what has driven you from your heavenly course? What occasion threw your horses from their reliable track? Surely the conquered Titans are not trying war once again now that the prison of Dis has been opened? Surely wounded Tityus does not renew that ancient wrath in his tired breast? Surely Typhon does not unfold his side from the mountain which he has cast off? Surely a high road is not constructed by the Phlegraen enemies and Thessalian Pelion is not pressed upon by the Thracian Ossa? Have the customary revolutions passed away? If nothing sets, will nothing rise?

The dewy mother of dawn, accustomed to hand the horses of the sun to the god, is stunned at the awry threshold of her kingdom. She does not know how to soak his weary team or how to plunge their manes, reeking with sweat, beneath the sea. The setting sun, himself an unaccustomed guest, sees Aurora, and he orders the darkness to rise while the night is not prepared: the stars do not climb, nor do the heavens flash with any fire; the grave moon does not scatter the shadows.

But whatever it is, may the night be here! Our hearts, stricken with fear, tremble; they tremble lest everything fall into fatal ruin, ugly chaos again overwhelm the gods and men, and nature again hide the lands, surrounding seas and roving stars of the painted world. Commanding time the leader of the stars will not give the signs of summer and winter with the rising of his eternal torch; the moon, not exposed to Phoebus's flames, will not take away the fears of the night, and she will not, running her shorter curved path, defeat her brother's reins. The crowd of the gods, pressed together, will go into hiding in one place.

This signal bearer for the long years who, traversable in the sacred heavens, carves a path curving the celestial zones with an oblique course, will see the fallen stars as it is falling; Aries the ram, who no longer sails back with kind spring with the warm west wind, will go headlong into the waves through which he had carried terrified Helle; this Taurus the bull, who displays the Hyades in his shining horn, will drag the twins Gemini and the claws of crooked Cancer; Herculean Leo, burning with blazing flames, again will fall from heaven; Virgo will fall into the abandoned lands, and the weights of just Libra will fall, and they will drag fierce Scorpio with them; and old Chiron, who holds his feathered arrows on his Harmonian bow string, will ruin his arrows with a broken bow string. Icy Capricorn, bringing back slow winter, will fall and break your urn, whoever you are; Pisces the last of the stars will die with you, and the sea, burying everything, will drown Ursa Major which has never been bathed in the sea; and sinuous as a river the Serpent, which divides the Bears, will fall, and Cygnus, the lesser, cold with stern frost, now joined to the great river will fall, and Arctophylax, the deliberate guard of his wagon, no longer stable will fall.

Do we, whom the world crushes beneath its overturned axis, seem worthy out of so great a people? Does the last age come upon us? O we have been created with this hard fate: we miserable ones have either lost the sun or driven it away. Let our complaints go away; depart, fear. Whoever is greedy for life does not wish to die while the world is perishing with him.

— Atreus

Chorus exits

Act V

V. i

Atreus and slaves in the royal palace

Atreus (*aside*): I, equal to the stars, even walk above them all as I touch the high pole with my haughty head. Now I hold the glory of the kingdom, the throne of my father. I dismiss the gods on high: I have achieved the end of my prayers; it is well, it is more than enough. Now it is even enough for me. But why should it be enough? I will proceed even though the father is satisfied with their corpses. The day retreats so that shame does not hinder me. Proceed while heaven is empty; indeed if only I was able to hold the fleeing gods and drag the company of them so that they would all see the banquet.—the let the fallen see: that is enough. Even though the day is unwilling, I will strike down the darkness, beneath which your miseries are hidden, for you. For too long you lie down as a guest with an untroubled and cheerful expression; now enough time has been given to the tables and enough to Bacchus: it is necessary for Thyestes to be sober for such evils.

(*to slaves*) You, crowd of slaves, loosen the gates of the temple; let the festive household be opened. It is pleasing for me to see, admiring the heads of his sons, what complexion he will wear, what words his grief will first pour out, or how his body, stunned, will grow rigid once his breath has been driven out. This is the fruit of my labor. I do not wish to see misery but misery while it is created.

(*The doors are opened and Thyestes is visible in the banquet hall*) The many opened roofs, shine with torchlight. He, himself lying with his belly up, lies on purple and gold while he props his head, heavy with wine, up with his left hand. He belches violently. O I am the most exalted of the gods of heaven and the king of kings! I have exceeded my vows. He is well-fed. He drinks undiluted wine from a large silver cup—do not refrain from your drink: even now so much of the blood of the sacrifices is left; the color of the old wine will hide this—let the meal be finished with this goblet. Let the father drink wine with the blood of his children mixed in: he would have drunk my own. Look! Now he calls for songs, and festive voices, and he hardly controls himself.

V. ii

Thyestes in the royal banquet hall

Thyestes: Hearts dulled with long evils, lay down your anxious concerns. Let grief and fear flee, and let poverty, the nervous companion of the sad exile, and shame, which is heavy in disastrous affairs, flee. It matters more from where you fall than to where. It is

43

a great thing, having fallen from a high peak, to fasten one's sure foot on a level place it is a great thing, having been crushed by a huge disordered heap of evils, to suffer the burdens of a broken kingdom with an unbent neck, and having been overcome by evils, to worthily endure imposed evils.

But now drive off the clouds of savage fate, and put away the marks of that whole miserable time; let pleasant expressions return to happy things; send the old Thyestes from your mind. Their own faults follow miserable ones so that they never believe happy things; although happy fortune returns, it disgusts the afflicted one to rejoice. Why do you recall me and forbid me to celebrate this festive day? Why do you order me to weep, O grief who rises without cause? Why do you forbid me to bind my hair with a pleasing blossom?

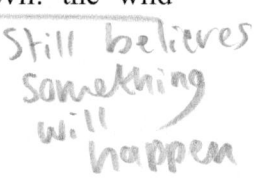

Forbids, it forbids! The spring flowers gradually fall from my head; my hair, wet with rich perfumes, has stood up among sudden terrors; rain falls from my unwilling face; a groan comes up in the middle of talking. Grief loves the usual tears; there is an ominous desire for weeping for the miserable. It pleases me to let loose inauspicious complaints; it pleases me to rend these garments dyed with Tyrian purple; it pleases me to shriek. The mind sends signs of future grief before its presaged evil: the wild storm presses upon the sailors when the calm waters swell without a wind.

What sorrows do you invent for yourself, or what disturbances do you create for yourself, foolish man? Hand over your trusting heart to your brother; now you fear whatever it is either without cause or too late. I do not wish to be unhappy, but roving terror wanders within; my eyes pour sudden tears, and is not the cause near at hand: is it sadness or fear? Or does great pleasure have tears?

V. iii

Atreus enters

Atreus: We celebrate a joyous day, brother, with mutual harmony: this is the day which creates a strong scepter and which solidifies a solid peace of sure trust.

Thyestes: An abundance of food and no less wine holds me. This final touch is able to add to my pleasure: if to rejoice with my sons is added to my happiness.

Atreus: Believe that here are your sons in the embrace of their father: here they are and will be. No part of your offspring will be taken away from you. I will provide the faces which you have longed for, and I will fill the whole father with his multitude. You will be satisfied lest you be afraid. Just now they, accompanied by my own children, are attending the pleasant sacrifices of the junior table, but they will be summoned. Take this cup filled with wine from the same family.

Thyestes: I claim the gift of my brother's feast. Let wine be poured out to the gods. Then let it be drunk. But what is this? My hands do not wish to obey; a weight rises, and it weighs down my right hand; the wine, which has been brought near to my very lips, flees, and it flows from my frustrated mouth around my jaws. It has leapt from the table itself to the trembling soil. The fire scarcely gives off light; in fact heaven itself, austere and forsaken, is paralyzed between day and night. What is this? More and more the dome of heaven sinks; a gloom thicker than dense shadows gathers, and night conceals itself in night. Every star flees; whatever it is I ask that it may spare my brother and children. Let the whole storm die on this cheap head. Return my children to me now.

Atreus: I will return them, and no day will snatch them from you.

Thyestes: What tumult disturbs my innards? What trembled within? I feel an unbearable burden, and my chest groans with a groan not my own. Be near, children; you unhappy father calls; be near! This pain will flee once you have been seen—from where do they interrupt?

Atreus: Father, prepare yourself for their embrace (*a platter with their heads and dismembered limbs is unveiled*) they have come; don't you recognize them at all?

Thyestes: I recognize my brother. Earth, you allowed him to bear such evil? You, having broken open, do not plunge to the Stygian underworld and its shadows, and you do not remove the kingdom with its king to the empty void? You do not, convulsing from the bottommost ground to the entire ceiling, destroy Mycenae? We each ought already to rest near Tantalus; once the bonds there and hear have been loosened, if there is any place lower than Tartarus, send our ancestor to this immense vale beneath your curved surface, and cover us, whom you have buried with the entire Acheron. Let criminal spirits wander above our heads and with its blazing sea let the Phlegethon, fiery and violent, driving all its sands, flow above our exile—does the earth lie unmoved like a spiritless bulk? The gods have fled.

Atreus: Now welcome them in a better manner, drinking those whom you've requested for a long time—there is no delay from your brother. Enjoy them; kiss them; divide your embraces between the three.

Thyestes: This is peace? This is goodwill? This is the confidence of a brother? This is how you lay aside hatred? I do not ask that I, their father, have my children unharmed; with the crime and hate intact, a brother asks his brother what is able to be given. Allow me to bury them; return that which you separated to be immediately burned. I, a father about to have nothing, ask for nothing but to be destroyed.

Atreus: You have whatever is left over from your sons, and you have whatever is not left over.

Thyestes: Do they lie either as fodder for the savage birds, or are they served to sea creatures, or do they feed the wild animals?

Atreus: You yourself have dined on your sons in an impious feast.

Thyestes: Is this what the gods were ashamed of; did this drive the day backward to the east? What cries or what complaints will I miserably give? What words will be sufficient for me? I examine their severed heads and their cut off hands and broken feet with their crushed legs—this is what a greedy father has not been able to grasp. They roll around within my innards, and the enclosed sin wrestles around without end, and it searches for an escape. Give me your sword, brother (that has much of my blood): let the road to my children be through a sword. Is your sword denied? My bruised chest will resound with crushing lamentation—hold your hand, unhappy one; let us yield to the shadows. Who has seen such evil? What Henochian living on the rough cliff of the inhospitable Caucuses, or what Procrustes, the dread of the Cecropian lands? Behold I, a father, oppress my sons, and I am oppressed by my sons—is there any limit of evil?

Atreus: There ought to be a limit to evil when you do evil not when you return it. This actually is a meager thing for me. I should have poured the hot blood from their wounds themselves into your throat so that you drank the blood of the living—while I rushed, I cheated my anger. I gave them wounds with firm steel; I cut them down at the altar; I appeased the altars with their consecrated gore, and carving their lifeless bodies, I tore the arms into little scraps, and I concealed these in the boiling lambs; I ordered that those drip into the low flames; I hewed off the limbs and muscles from your living sons, and I saw that their entrails, transfixed on the slender spit, bellowed, and I myself built up the flames with my own hand—yet their father was able to have done all those things better: my pain has fallen in vain: he tore his sons with his impious mouth yet while he was unaware and while they were unaware.

Thyestes: Listen, you seas closed up by the wandering shores, and you gods, also listen to this evil deed, wherever you have fled; listen to it, dead ones. Hear it lands and Tartarean night, oppressive and dark with mist; be free from our voices (I have been abandoned by you; you alone see my misery who have also been forsaken by the stars.) I will offer no wicked offerings; I will plead for nothing for myself—and what can be asked on my behalf? My prayers will be offered for you all. You, the greatest ruler of heaven, the powerful lord of the heavenly kingdom, roll up the white world in frightful clouds; begin the wars of the winds, and strike with thunder the violent everywhere. And do not attack the buildings and homes with that lesser hand and javelin but with that hand by which the triple mountains and the giants who stand equal to the mountains fell; set loose these arms, and hurl your fires. Avenge the lost day; hurl your flames; fil up the light which has been stolen away, with your lightning bolts. So that you do not hesitate for any longer, let the evil cause be each of us; if this is not enough, let the evil be mine.

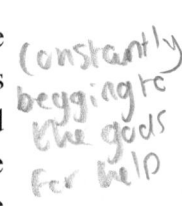

Strike me; send your flaming brand with its three-pronged javelin into this chest. If I, their father, wish to inter my children and hand them over to the final fire, I must be burned. If nothing moves the gods above and no god attacks the wicked with bolts, let eternal night endure, and let it cover the immeasurable evil deeds with long gloom, and I do not protest, titan, if you persist.

Atreus: Now I praise my hands; now my true reward has been acquired. If you had not suffered thusly, I would have wasted the evil deed. Now I believe that the children are born to me; now I believe that trust is restored to the marital bed.

Thyestes: Why did my children deserve this?

Atreus: Because they had been yours.

Thyestes: Sons to their father—

Atreus: I confess that what also delights me is that they are certainly yours.

Thyestes: I swear that the gods are the guardians of the pious.

Atreus: Why not marriages?

Thyestes: Who repays wickedness with wickedness?

Atreus: I know what you are complaining about: because the wicked deed was claimed first, you are troubled, and it does not trouble you because you swallowed the wicked feast but because you were not preparing it. You had intended to serve similar foods to an ignorant brother and to attack his children with the assistance of their mother and to scatter them in a similar death. This one thing hindered you: you thought that they were yours.

Thyestes: The gods will be near as our protectors; my prayers will deliver you, who are about to be punished, to them.

Atreus: I hand you, who are soon to be punished, over to your children.

Printed in Great Britain
by Amazon